Wakefield Press

Farmwoman

Ray Tyndale came to South Australia from England in 1970. Past lives have seen her run a farm, bring up a family, direct an a cappella group, and work variously as cook, brickie, truckie, economist, accountant, gardener, psychologist and bookbinder. All of this rich life experience, and more, informs her poetry.

Lately, Ray has been exploring the Australian Outback, not only enjoying hilarious and intrepid adventures, but also looking more carefully into the role of women in the bush today. Ray has been awarded a doctorate in Creative Writing.

Also by Ray Tyndale

Sleeping Under a Grand Piano: Ten South Australian Poets, 1999
Friendly Street New Poets Six, 2000
Pastorale, 2004
maiden voyage, 2005
Sappho at Sixty, 2007

Farmwoman

Celebrating old friendships!

with warm wishes,

Ray Tyndale

Ray

Wakefield Press

Wakefield Press
1 The Parade West
Kent Town
South Australia 5067
www.wakefieldpress.com.au

First published December 2007
Copyright © Ray Tyndale, 2007

All rights reserved. This book is copyright. Apart from any fair dealing for the purposes of private study, research, criticism or review, as permitted under the Copyright Act, no part may be reproduced without written permission. Enquiries should be addressed to the publisher.

Edited by Bethany Clark, Wakefield Press
Cover designed by Liz Nicholson, designBITE
Designed and typeset by Clinton Ellicott, Wakefield Press
Printed and bound by Hyde Park Press, Adelaide

National Library of Australia
Cataloguing-in-publication entry

Author: Tyndale, Ray R. (Ray Rosalind)
Title: Farmwoman/author, Ray Tyndale.
Publisher: Kent Town, S. Aust.: Wakefield Press, 2007.
ISBN: 978 1 86254 766 7 (pbk.)
Dewey Number: A821.4

Publication of this book was assisted by the Commonwealth Government through the Australia Council, its arts funding and advisory body.

To the hardworking women who contribute valiantly to the running of Australian farms, who have been generous to me with their personal stories.

Author's Note

A version of this work was presented towards a PhD in Creative Writing at the University of Adelaide, which was granted in 2004. I acknowledge and am grateful for a partial scholarship to complete the doctorate, from the University of Adelaide Scholarship Fund. I also acknowledge with thanks funding from ArtsSA, for both a mentorship with Canberra poet Geoff Page and an editing mentorship with visiting New York editor Robert B. Wyatt.

Thanks also to Eva Sallis, Bob Wyatt, Geoff Page, Peggy Mares, Anne Bartlett, Cathy McGowan, Nick Jose, Heather Kerr and to all those unnamed women out there on the land – you know who you are, and I salute you.

I

I

if I could speak out loud   speak my mind   if I
could say anything that would be listened to   if I
could just open my mouth and let words fall out
if I could only say what is on my mind but I can't
here in this stuffy farm kitchen not a breath of air
moving the doors all wide open the air as hot and thick
outside as in   here in this farm kitchen sitting around
the table where I serve meal after meal day after day
week in week out
here around the well-scrubbed table on the old wooden
chairs that have done service for farm generations
painted and stripped and repainted   repaired and
re-glued repainted and stripped   stiff backed and
unrelenting as the seasons and the cropping and the
bank
each has a voice which will be listened to but me
each can say their piece   I am the outsider   I am
the daughter-in-law   the bushie   *dumbo*   I
wasn't born on the family farm
one day I will say it all

2

a little girl helping my Gran   I remember vividly
though she died forty years ago   I set the scrubbed
deal table for breakfast with white pottery bowls
the heavy blue and white milk jug filled with scalded
milk and covered with beaded lace   the treacle tin
loaf of bread ready to be buttered and sliced   /only
Gran ever wielded the bread knife/
an assortment of spoons   big brown pot of dripping
honeycomb on a saucer   I waited at her elbow for
instructions
she stopped stirring the porridge on the blackened top
of the wood stove   she stood with the wooden spoon
in her right hand   her old body rigid and angular
with the urgency of her words   *actions speak*
louder than words Molly my girl   *never mind if the*
cat's got your tongue   *you just show them what a*
sensible little thing you are   *they'll take note of you*
you mark my words

3

I learnt to toddle among the chooks   I learnt to fend
off the rooster with his sharp fighting spur   my
water play grew from chook trough to duck pond to
dam with the geese and on to the creek which wound
down through the valley of the farm
Mum kept chooks for pin money before the Egg Board
made it hard   the bantam hens   /smaller and
more showy than the layers/   were always ready to
ruffle up   they'd brood up to two dozen eggs at a
time and be spitfire little mothers to the balls of fluff in
the home paddock   scratching Mum as she up-
ended the chicks to sex them   *these for layers*
these to be fattened as meat birds   *see here Molly*
can you see these are the little boys?   the difference
never obvious to me

meat chickens were kept in a big barn and fed grains
and kale and corncobs from the vegie garden   layers
roamed all day across the home paddocks scratching for
seeds and bugs but at night they went willingly to roost
on perches   huddled together for comfort in the
fox-proof shedding

4

Mum taught me to throw out the wheat to the chooks
    to keep the drinking water clean   to collect the
eggs warm from laying   holding my pinny up in my
left hand and carrying the precious hoard carefully into
the musty underground pantry   /dug into the
hillside behind the kitchen/   together we would set
the eggs round-end-up in layers of cardboard
twenty-eight   twenty-nine   thirty to a layer
ready for market on Friday
Mum and Gran and I pulled the feathers off the
headless meat chickens   the air nosecurling with
burnt feather and wet chook   Dad covered in blood
all appetite gone for a day or so
death always hovering

5

I must have been born in the dairy   can't remember
not being around cows   knee-high to a chicken I fed
the newborn calves   taken from their mothers after
their first feed   warm milk from a bottle   sticking
my fingers into their soft mouths   their tongues suck
and rasp
taller now   feeding eight calves at a time from
the milk churn fitted with ten black rubber teats
/the ten-titted cow Dad called it/
the calves no longer gentle   splayed around the
churn like the spokes of a cartwheel   pushing each
other off the teats in their eagerness   round and
round   their tails in a wrigglefrenzy
soon they had names and took their turn in the dairy

6

I cried for the tottering bull calves   packed off in the
butcher's truck the day after they were born   some
even picked straight out of the paddock   their cords
still soft and drippy   their mothers bellowing
frantically over the fence
I learnt to harden my heart
and my stomach also   watching Dad kill our mutton
sometimes a hand-reared wether for a special Sunday
roast
leaning   /elbows on the table/   seeing how Mum
cut up the carcass   how the pet lamb in the home
paddock which had followed at my heels turned into
chops and kidneys and roast

7

Uncle John was my special friend   he came whenever
there was machinery to be repaired   the best bush
mechanic in the state Dad reckoned   he would come
for weeks at a time and tinker around all day in the
sheds then bunk down in the shearers' hut
Uncle John ate with us in the big farm kitchen then he
would sit me on his lap and read me stories and
sometimes he would bath me out in the washhouse
he tickled me and made me laugh   he showed me
how to feel hot and tingly with my fingers in my body
in his lap being dried   we rocked together singing
happy songs and he went red in the face
Uncle John said   *this is our secret Molly   mind you
don't let the cat out of the bag as that will spoil it*   I
didn't know what our secret was but I liked the way he
made me laugh so I didn't tell anyone   I didn't want to

spoil the secret so I stopped talking   Dad said *where's my little chatterbox?*   I laughed and I listened but I didn't let on   I listened when they said Uncle John   /they called him John the mechanic/   they said John had been interfering with little girls and had gone to Gaol it said so in the paper   I thought Gaol must be a long way away because he never came back   I missed Uncle John but I never told our secret
I became silent

8

silent as a child   as a daughter   as a playmate
our quiet little Molly-coddle   our dark horse
our dumbo   silence in a growing girl is taken for
insolence   for stupidity   for having secrets
I'd always been quiet but now silent at the dinner table
silent on the school bus   silent at the back of class
silent in the bullying the taunting and the sidelining
silent in the questioning   silent

but the animals could talk to me and I could talk to
them   quiet crooning song   intimate
endearments   songs of love   *here chooky
chookies*   *g'day Bluey g'day Ned*   *well my lovely
moos*   *how are you today?*
no one like Molly can get the cows to let their milk
down   Molly has a way with those dogs   Molly
is a wizard in the dairy   Molly'll make a great
farmer's wife   won't answer back

9

Dad caught trout in the creek   in green waders to his
armpits he walked up Buckland Creek flicking his rod
with the fly he had bent over for hours the previous
night   tiny colourful feathers   *a tantalising
morsel*   two big trout were more than enough
for a meal for him and Mum   Gran and me   fried
in a dry frypan sprinkled with salt
I would lie on the flat black rocks at the edge of the
creek   water over my elbows   wiggling my
fingers like spiders until the speckled trout would let me
touch them   shimmering in the crinkly sunlight
/the sun shone all the time/

Dad said I could take the trout by surprise with my
tickling and grab it out of the water   but I didn't

if I rolled over and stared upwards I could see the sky
through overhanging silver aspen leaves   sometimes
clouds

10

to be silent as a child was not hard   not for me
my world was full of noise   no need for words
words turned noise into soundshriek   the dogs
barked   /yelped when I rode them/   panted
great slobbery breaths after racing up the rocky hillside
farm machinery rattled and growled when it worked
and when it didn't Dad would tinker and swear   the
magpies in the morning made me long for a voice like
theirs
I practiced quietly up on the hillside   singing gently
rocking   rocking
Mum and Dad grew used to my silence   startled as I
was if it broke
we were a quiet family

11

Mum didn't talk much to Dad   and Dad didn't talk much to Mum   as if they didn't need to   after Gran died when I was little they became quieter   a friendly silence and comfortable   easy with each other   no need to shout either   my silence not remarkable   they yarned with friends and neighbours   I liked to listen   there was plenty of laughter in the quietness

12

Meg and Rosy were my childhood playmates   one
lanky as a tomato stake the other plump and giggly and
full of ideas   unfazed by my silence   we boosted
the school numbers from twelve to fifteen when we
started together   Miss Anderson had *more mischief
on her hands*   there were never more than sixteen
all the way through that tiny one-roomed school and
only Miss Anderson to teach us   I never think of
school with unhappiness   I think of skipping on the
long rope   lunch under the peppertree
tadpoles in Fowlers jars   in the summer holidays the
kids mostly went on camp to Portsea   meeting
others from little schools in country Victoria   Mum
and Dad couldn't afford for me to go

I don't suppose I would have liked it anyway   the
other children said the sea was big and cold and made
them shiver   they drew pictures of big ships sailing
past with white lifeboats and smoke coming out of
funnels

but high school was less happy   we travelled a long
way down the valley on the school bus and were all
three of us targeted   *cocky kids*   *peasants*   *tit
tuggers*   and me especially   *dumbo*

13

out of school we did everything together   me and
Meg and Rosy   acting out scary bits of The
Phantom in the forest   sliding down steep grassy
paddocks on sheets of cardboard   tumbles and
prickles and barbed wire   chalking up hearts and
initials of boys   /real and imagined/   on the back
walls of farm sheds   risking the snakes in the long
grass   taking all our clothes off to swim in the creek
shrieking with the possibility that boys might see us
might see the little growing knobs on our chests
might see the little wisps of hair   might see

14

sometimes I went to Meg's house for tea
sometimes Rosy's   sometimes they both came to
my house and Mum would bake special things for us
chocolate crackles   oat fingers that we called
scranchum because they were crunchy and sweet
once a square cake covered in marzipan that her
mother used to make   her own mother not Gran
Gran was my only gran
Meg's house was calm and tidy   set in the middle of
an ordered apple orchard   a big red International
truck parked inside the orderly shed   'Wilson and
Son'   the sign on the truck door said before
Jim had completed primary school
Meg's mother taught chemistry at our secondary
school   Myrtleford High   Meg's house was full of

books which were always available to me   my Mum
and Dad with no time for books   always flat out
working the farm   always scratching

books on science and philosophy   Bertrand
Russell's *Principia Mathematica* with his picture on
the inside back cover   he looked like one of our
roosters   gardening books and travel by women to
exotic places with Bedouin Sherpas   Red Indians
for guides   and donkeys   camels   llamas to
ride and unmentionable toilet facilities   women in
bulky Victorian dresses   how did they piss?
not a question to ask Meg's mother

15

Rosy's house was chaotic   a tumble of unruly children   wild gardens full of organic vegetables long before they were fashionable   Rosy's dad would come to our dairy with an old squeaky wheelbarrow   its metal wheel buckled and wobbly cart off the slurry from the cows   almost licking his lips with delight   household scraps would be interred with reverence   the whole family part of the ritual of digging and planting   growing and eating Rosy's mum's head would appear above the sweet corn or silverbeet   the celeriac or the artichokes pretty blue bee balm or cherry rhubarb   pushing stray dark streamers of hair from her eyes   dirty but beaming

always welcoming and easy   not needing me to
chatter   plenty of chatter in that family
Reds   my Dad chuckled but never stopped me going
Rosy's dad always had a fag attached to his bottom lip
it never fell out   shop steward in a milk factory or a
timber mill when he had work   not often
Mum would send me down to their ramshackle cottage
with new-laid eggs   fresh milk in a billy
forequarter chops when we'd killed   they were a
happy mob   I loved going there   we played pick-
up-sticks on their big kitchen table   all leaning over
and trying to breathe the sticks to budge   knuckle
bones and hopscotch   tag and even postman's knock

16

then Mum died   just suddenly   didn't say she felt sick   just sighed and keeled over in the kitchen early one morning   I hadn't thought how much work she did until I had to do it before and after school   she always was quiet   Mum was

17

Dad needed my help in the dairy   I had to get up so
early   what with the chooks and geese   and
taking such ages to get to and from school   it
became hard staying awake in lessons   Dad said I
could leave school if I wanted   work full-time on the
farm   I would've   but I was doing well at school
would miss my friends
Dad was already talking of selling up   no son to
inherit   I didn't know to argue

18

when Mum died   I used to think   out there in
the dairy   or getting dinner for just Dad and me
or sitting staring at my homework but not seeing a word
of it
I used to think   did she know about my secret?
so quiet herself   did she sometimes wonder   she
said nothing when my periods started   she asked no
questions   I didn't pester her with adolescent
concerns   didn't have many really   did she worry
did I kill her with my silence?
I wanted to talk to her

19

Meg's mother encouraged us into science   all three
of us working together   most children already back
on the farm
now we travelled into Wangaratta every day for senior
school   no demand for matriculation at Myrtleford
High   Meg's mother set us challenging homework
Rosy's mum and dad were all for *education for the workers*
my Dad watched with a kind of puzzled amusement
proud of his only child   the silent child bright
enough to matriculate
Meg's mother suggested university   Meg had
decided to be a teacher like her mum   Rosy wanted
to do voluntary service overseas   in Ethiopia or Peru
preferably a war-torn country   always a romantic
our Rosy

I fancied being a vet eventually   liked being around
animals

I topped my class   got a shire scholarship   no
one more surprised than me   the University of
Melbourne accepted all three of us   to live in St
Hilda's College
I'd never been out of the valley

20

I missed the cows when I went to Melbourne Uni   I
missed my home   I missed my Dad   I ached for
the valley   its lush meadow hay   bubbling trout
streams   forested rolling hilltops   many times in
the first year I thought I must go home to the farm
but Meg and Rosy were at college with me   we had
such fun   real department stores instead of the Myers
catalogue   cinemas   milk bars with huge servings
of chocolate milkshake   scholarship meant I didn't
have much to spend but it was all so different   I was
used to making a little go a long way

21

Dad wrote me that he'd sold the farm   *Oh Dad   I wish you hadn't   I would have liked to*   I guess he wanted a son to work the farm with him   of course I didn't say

then he wrote that he was going steady with Aunt Ada   *who?*   then he'd moved in with her in Wodonga   they'd set up a little florist's business together   I stayed with them in the holidays   it wasn't like the farm   not like home   Aunt Ada kept trying to catch me out   *see   I knew you could talk   just need a bit of practice lovey*

22

I did what everyone did at uni   I went to parties
I studied hard   I met Dave at the Melbourne branch
of Rural Youth   had to keep some connection with
the land   Meg and I both enjoyed Rural Youth
meeting other people off farms   Meg went out with
Dave first   then he was intrigued by quiet me
Dave was studying economics   hating it but
enjoying his freedom   I might have wondered about
that
I went to folk nights at the pub   I learnt my way
round on public transport

so I got my Science degree   I got my farmer   I
got pregnant   to a red-headed farm boy   in
silence mostly   I'd got so used to being quiet

II

23

I knew about sex   Uncle John had been a good
teacher   anyway I was surrounded by it on the
farm   roosters rough-housing the hens   then the
communal dust bath   Benny our enormous almost
black Friesian bull was daily courted and humped by
the herd   when he   /in turn/   found a
receptive cow he followed her for hours   salivating
licking her swollen vulva   putting up his broad head
and bulling   savouring the air she walked through
then up he would go his forelegs scrabbling for a
foothold on her back slobber drifting from his open

jaws his long thin pointed red penis jabbing jabbing
she soon back to quiet grazing   the germ of the next
year's milking already growing
I asked no questions about sex   about touching
about loving and touching and passion and arching my
back and touching   about losing myself   about
throbbing and burning about crying out in ecstasy
no one told me about crying out

24

I could not know   when I gave myself to Dave I could not know what that meant for my future   how could I know that I was giving myself body and soul to his family   his farm   as well as to his insistent provocative desire   in the sweat of the sheets I could not see the domination of his parents   in the slippery coming and going I did not think in terms of other people's farmland   other people's homesteads other people's ways of doing things   in the scratch of the fingernails down flushed skin I did not recognise the sharpness of my loss

25

when he took me in college he knew I wasn't dumb
when he whispered sweet nothings he knew I could
whisper them back   but when he took me to his
family I was dumbstruck   I carried the seed of their
next generation but they misunderstood my silence for
insolence

I have married his family and they do not want me and
I stand mute before their dislike
a boy must sow his oats but he shouldn't have got her in the
family way   she hasn't got any land   what's her
family?   any number of nice girls just waiting to be asked
should have kept him on the farm   well what's done is done
I have kept quiet for so long that I don't know what to
say

26

our new home is the sprawling homestead   nothing's
done to acknowledge the change in his status   or
mine   he has to ask for the money to buy a double
bed   we squeeze with silent laughter into his old
single until it arrives on a Co-op truck from Wangaratta

can you milk?   asks the sister-in-law looking at me
sideways not to meet my glance   I nod   so does
she in the direction of the dairy   she can spend more
time off the farm   escape to city cafes   in my
smiling pleasure at getting my own dairy again she sees
an ally within this tough family   she doesn't appear
to dislike me   I'm useful to her

you can cook   says the mother-in-law leading me to the wood stove   *the meat's hanging*   *the wood's in the tank behind the old dunny*   *breakfast at seven*   *smoko at ten*   *dinner at twelve thirty*   *smoko at three*   *tea at six*   *supper at nine*   I love cooking   she hates it   she'll have more time to embroider   she does exquisite cross-stitch   we'll rub along OK   I've almost forgotten what it's like   to have a mother   she's never had a daughter   only the wives of her sons

now I'm here   the women are no longer outnumbered

she a good lay?   leers the hog of an elder brother Chris

I'll have to watch that one

27

doesn't take me long to see Chris's frustrations
generations of expectation laid on the eldest son to
produce sons for the farm   but his wife seems unable
to enter into the spirit   keeps miscarrying and Chris
hates farming   he will inherit the gracious old
homestead but he and his wife like modern things and
privacy   a pregnant healthy farm girl on the arm of
his young brother is an unbearable provocation

28

no privacy on the family farm   and no lying in bed
of a morning   sex becomes furtive   both of us
silent   the joy we had in each other threatens to
unwind   my bridal mistakes in the unfamiliar kitchen
are hard to bear
the undercooked roast not laughed away   the runny
jelly a shouting matter
I am not used to   our home hadn't worked in this
way and no one ever shouted   Dave's dad doesn't
swear   he shouts and gets his own way   he doesn't
like me   finds my silence as threatening as I find his
shouting
this family is like a farmyard and he's the cock of the
heap   I'm at the bottom as new wife of second son
if I don't rock the boat   keep quiet and work well I
might change things round here   quietly though
I won't deny he's a good farmer

Dave's mum   /Mother I have to call her/   loses
no opportunity for spite   sharp little digs about my
cooking   about the baby   trapping her son into
marriage   about my so-called progressive ideas
trying to spend all their hard earned money   I just
wanted to try some fruit trees or some rare breed
chooks   showing my *blockie* upbringing   I'm
easily silenced   my silence infuriates

29

I hunger for words to slide off the page and into my
mouth   there I would control the flow as with an
irrigation valve   /tight shut for secrets/   a quarter
turn for everyday conversation   *have you fed the dogs*
I feel sick   *shall we go to bed?*
half cock for careful instructions   to mix a hazardous
pesticide   *have you filled the tank?*   *don't bat an*
eyelid at the calf auction   another quarter turn of the
valve into an easy camaraderie   a gossip   a phone
link
unwound to fully open   the valve will vomit the
complete drama queen   gunning for attention and
holding the weekly meeting of the farm family
spellbound   the cat out of the bag
but not yet

30

in the dairy they can't find fault and I increase the yield
within weeks   I scrub and sweep and polish and
disinfect until the whole dairy is spotless and stays that
way   the milk truck driver never kept waiting
the books all in order   soon the mating charts are left
to me
I come to the dairy when things are tough and Dave
knows he can find me here alone   the rich cuddy
smell of the cows as comforting as the familiarity of his
body   this is not what he had imagined in college
nor me   he sees now he will always be the second
son   his brother who hates the farm will inherit it
because he was born first and that's how it is and always
will be amen   primogeniture rules

his sister-in-law who wants the city will have the
homestead   we will always be second best   but
loyal

it's not hard to love this farm with its always green valley
and forested hilltops   trout streams and waterholes
good rainfall and all   perfect for dairying

31

this farm I've married into is not like the one I grew up
on   a constant struggle with marginal land high up
in the valleys   we were happy and had enough to
get by
this farm has been in the family for over a hundred years
has expanded with each generation   now it's nearly
ten times bigger than ours was

32

the homestead and sheds are on the Dairy Block east of
the river   first Australian soil for many postwar
European migrants branching out from Bonegilla
Dave's family was here long before   they would have
ousted Indigenous owners   no doubt without
conscience   *terra nullius*   had the pick of the land
eight hundred acres of rich river flat with water
meadows for the milkers   higher ground for weaners
and dry cows

forested hilltops owned by the state for logging   big
old gum trees long gone   now patterned with
interwoven pine and regrowth   the pine dark-green
diamonds among the grey bush   logging trucks
/driven by Czechs   Latvians   Georgians   *Balts*
Dave's dad and plenty others call them/   churning
up the hill roads   grinding of gears in the still air

33

meadow hay cut in October   the air sharp with
pollen and grass seed   some hay baled and stored in
hay sheds   some sold   some for storing in the two
big silage pits dug into the hillside behind the
homestead   not too close   it smells ripe as it
settles   the riper the better for the cows   they
love it best of all
several miles of river frontage for trout fishing rights and
unlimited water   the clear fast water lined with aspen
willow eaten off to cow height like trees in a child's
farmyard set   but good shade   room for twenty or
more cows under swaying tendrils   chewing the cud
chewing   chewing   I'm sure those cows are
thinking

34

thirteen hundred acres up the valley   the Hill
Paddocks for merinos   triticale for the piggeries
wild ponies brought down from the High Country by
leather-brown horsemen to be quietened for a life of
pony clubs and sugar lumps   Dave is a wizard with
those horses   talks to them like I sing to the cows
by the time children come wide-eyed to choose one
they're as docile and gentle as any mum could wish
still with the fire of the wild to add a sparkle to
ownership   pretty horses ready to be named *Blaze* or
Striker or   /of course/   *Black Beauty*   high-
stepping from birth on mountainsides   rough manes
and sturdy

35

two and a half thousand flat dry acres out west beyond
Benalla   two big grain paddocks   no water
no power   no living
when first he brought me home   grown accustomed
to his freedom at university   Dave was brazen
enough to ask for a house to be built out on The Flat
not pouring money into bricks and mortar boy   running a
business here you know   not welfare   plenty of room in
the homestead   which is true
in the homestead they've got us where they can see us
at least I have two other women around to keep the
house clean

36

how will the next generation add to the landholding?
a tradition to maintain   I'm full of bright modern
ideas but am not heard   if Dave puts forward my
ideas   /shaped to his own design but mine to start
with/   he is mocked

*been getting ideas from that bush housewife of yours   let's
hear that you learned something at that university   cost us
enough to send you there   where's your broader vision
where're your management skills   push the farm forwards
boy   not back into the hill country*

I may not be able to contribute land but I can produce
the next generation   more than my poor sister-in-law
can
the brother-in-law uses her sterility as an excuse for
trying to feel me up whenever he can   he can't
possibly find me attractive in this condition   I can't
even see my own feet

37

I wanted my mother when I went into labour   little
local hospital in Beechworth   knew all the nurses
Clara Jones the midwife had been visiting for months
teaching me how to breathe for the different stages of
labour   watching my diet
Meg was with me   men were kept out of the labour
ward but Dave felt squeamish anyway   heaven knows
he's pulled enough animals into this world

38

Meg knew about this baby from the start   Meg was
Dave's girlfriend before me   those college days were
great   /miss the freedom   love marriage to a
good man   love having my own dairy/

I knew what it was   the pain of birth   I had
helped many cows as they fought to expel   had seen
the magic of dawning life   crooned with the mother
at the newborn calf in the blood-spattered hay   had
helped my sister-in-law as she bent double with the pain
of yet another miscarriage
but this time   this first time just for me   I wanted
my mother

III

39

at this moment as I push and scream   yes scream
this silent one screams for her mother   I want my
mother   I want   I don't want   help me   I
can't   Oh Mum

I have a son   a fine son   the first grandson for the
farm

40

motherhood is great   oh and the feel and the smell
of that fuzzy head nuzzled into my shoulder   now I
know why the cows mother-murmur to their calves
now I feel guiltier taking away their calves after twenty-
four hours   when I hold my boy

my Sam goes everywhere with me   in his bassinet in
the kitchen while I cook and in his bouncer in the
sunshine while I weed the vegetables and in a pouch on
my tummy when I bring in the cows   I can't bear to
be parted from him
the family want him called Richard after his grandfather

but I don't want him branded 'Dick'   I want to
call him Samson   to grow strong and tall   a
golden boy   he is christened Richard David
to me he will always be Sam   at least they didn't
want him to be John

41

we chattered to each other   Sam and I   when no
one else was around   I had no secrets from my baby
crooning happy little songs   mother songs
singing to my baby

my little family grew and still we chattered   Sam and
Robbie chattered to each other as they grew
Sally chattered with Sam and Robbie as she grew
three lovely babies   all close   all with variations of
their father's lovely curly pink-champagne hair
/will they hate me drawing attention to it as much as he
does   I wonder/

my silence in the world must have been like my own
mother's quietness was to me   an unremarkable
intimacy   comfortable   no need to share my
secret with my children

42

when I tell Dave my secret   /it's not a secret when
it's told/   Dave is so angry with John   but I don't
want him to be angry with John   I want him to be
angry with me   for not trusting him with my secret
earlier in our life together   as if I was scared
whether he would still love me
but you were just a little girl   but I enjoyed it I say
he was my special friend   I didn't know I was
supposed to feel violated so I didn't
his arms around me now in the quietness of the dairy
/we still have all our intimate times in the dairy/
you stay as quiet as you like my love   but no one   no
one gets anywhere near my daughter
Dave needs to be a strong dependable man   he gets a
rough time of it   on the farm

43

Dave does most of the work around the farm   and I
do the rest   until the children are big enough to
pitch in   Dave's father tells him what to do   he knows
perfectly well for himself but he lets his dad be in
control   Father thinks he is still boss while enjoying
his game of bowls in Beechworth
Dave's brother Chris disappears off shooting   says he's
going out to The Flat but he rarely does any work there
other than at seeding or harvest   spends most of his
time down the pistol club   or the pub
Dave's mum holds the purse strings   she clutches
them tightly to her chest   and she's tight
Dave doesn't grumble   neither do I   we just get
on with it   farming's like that   what with the
seasons and the weather and the markets   not much
point grumbling about family as well   some things
you just can't change

44

thank goodness for breasts   I lay down the fencing
pliers out of Robbie's reach   lift up my shirt and feed
my red-faced babe   in the sudden sucking silence
contemplating the satisfactory gleam of a new sheep
fence   the Hill Paddocks are a great place to work
in autumn   bronze tinge of turning leaves
lighting up the valley below like evening sun on water
my new daughter's soft wisps of red-tinged hair lift
gently in the warm April breeze   eyes closed
/her pleasure joining mine/   my carrot-topped
toddler at my feet   deeply immersed in a tumbling
tower of pebbles and mud
farm work doesn't wait for motherhood

45

one year when my babies were still small   we tried
some young heifers in one of the Hill Paddocks   one
year when water was short   the water meadows
needed it all to keep the milk yield up   the heifers
sickened quickly   drooping their heads   not
feeding   we tethered them instead along the
roadside
one poor little one   *Loppy Lugs* the kids called her
with her sad drooping ears   wound her rope around
and around   shorter and shorter against the star
dropper   lay down and stayed down   couldn't
budge her
cows in the paddock over the fence lowed in distress
they knew death   did they smell it?

at the post-mortem with the vet   puddling around in
her insides   the flesh pockmarked with bracken fern
poisoning   lucky we only lost one
didn't I tell you the Hill Paddock's no good for beasts?
Father shouted
hard to bear when he's right

46

sometimes I pause as the shadow lines elongate across
the Home Paddock   the sun a pale battery hen's egg
nudging the horizon   backlighting the clump of
scribbly gums   pasted as an afterthought onto the
bare paddock
I stand   hand to my eyes   squinting to catch the
last drops of daylight
then I fling my dairywoman's voice to the machinery
sheds   to the green hillside behind the homestead
to the empty silage pit   calling my light-foot children
to their tea   I wouldn't live anywhere else

47

once at school the children have to get used to loss of
freedom   growing up they go everywhere with us
childcare is the latest catchcry of women   it won't
happen in the bush   always watching nonstop for
our kids   so many dangers   rivers   dams
silos   to drown in   machinery to fall off or
under   sprays to drink   and gunshot never far
from our minds

Dave joined the search for a neighbour's youngest child
missing only an hour or two   they'd called all over
the farm   phoned all the surrounding farms
checked the school   post office   the local store
*must be here somewhere   can't have gone far   only
popped inside for a second*

twenty-three men left their work to comb the paddocks
before little Damien floated to the surface of the dam
he was only four   the whole district grieved
how easy it would be   it could happen to any of us

but when the children all go to school   just a little
local primary   I miss them with me as I work

48

Sam is first to go to school   he loves the chance to
brag and make new mates even though he's grown up
with most of the other kids   some new hobby farm
kids coming through though   he likes to think he
knows all about farming and can show off   him with
his red hair and his temper to match   gets into a few
fights   those city kids know a thing or two   he
never says   but sometimes I have to wash bloodspots
off his shirt

one by one I lose my babies to the education system
at least I can relax my vigilance during the week
they all have my large build and their father's hair
and Sam and Sally have tempers to match   maybe
they've inherited more from their grandfather than I
realised   Dave is as mild as a spring day and has
never laid a finger on them in spite of his own father's
urging

49

the extra labour on Thursdays   around the mundane milking chores   fifty pasties for tuck shop on Friday homegrown vegies minced the night before   the meat from the latest menopausal cow   /we eat all our own meat   cows and weaners come home from the slaughter house in cardboard boxes   straight into the new freezer   saves Dave a job he hated and me a lot of cutting up/   the pastry thrown together in the Sunbeam   all the lighter for the careless custom one and a half pasties for each child plus the Principal two teachers and a teacher's aide   each pasty with tomato sauce from a squeezie bottle   brown paper bag

enough funny-face cupcakes to feed an army   they
all get eaten
three of us mothers raising money for books for the
library   a child starving in Somalia   sick kids in
Chernobyl   the cause of the moment
time gossiping in the tuck shop every bit as precious
swapping dress patterns   recipes   remedies for
childhood ailments

50

I've seen ads in the *Women's Weekly* with shapely women
pumping iron in the gym to develop their abs and their
pecs   all kitted out in high-cut lycra   their legs
waxed to the bikini line   their make up on
I think to myself   they should come out here and
have dust brown legs without need for sunlamps
bulging muscles from pumping diesel   fifty-eight
hand pumps to fill the ute to go to the calf auction
no need for the bikini line either   or the make-up
no one takes a second look

51

townies   seeing me once a month in Wodonga for
the grocery shopping   a trip to the library   maybe
the doctor
see a caricature of myself dressed in my best clothes
sheer stockings   Fletcher Jones skirt   the pearls
Dad gave me for my twenty-first   one of those nice
shirts with plaid collar and cuffs
they see a woman who isn't there   townies know the
legend   Tammie Fraser   the myth of squattocracy
of landownership   townies see me as idle   rich
as stuck up
I can't sell the farm to come to town   can't come in
my everyday mucky-been-on-the-quad jeans and
sweat-stained T-shirt   down at heel one-pair-lasts-
for-years Blundstones   anyway Dave wouldn't let

me out of the gate looking like that
I'm fit because I work hard   brown from fresh air
I wish they'd see the real me

52

I enjoy the drive into town   very little traffic on our
narrow roads   time to catch the views   and my
breath
each time I go into Wodonga or Wangaratta I see the
changes   new forests planted   bits of gravel road
graded   houses and sheds going up on hobby blocks

how the family sneers at the hobby farms   maybe
people don't realise what a hard life it is out here   get
a bit of a rosy view from those eco magazines and then
let the land run down   not bred for it   they pay
good money for the land though
hobby farmers plant interesting crops   often make a
fist of it   at least they try   walnuts that will take
ten to fifteen years to come into bearing   cherries on
a slope they'll never get a tractor up   bronze

sculptures of horses galloping   look almost real in
the paddock   gave me a shock first time I saw them
with coloured sheep grazing among their hooves
snotty-nosed kids running bare and barefoot   happy
though   healthy
we avoid change in the country   hobby farmers
unsettle us
I drive with my head over one shoulder   as do all
farmers   got to see what the others are up to

53

on a shuddering indrawn breath the old pump down by
the river wheezes into action   as the clean cold water
is sucked up the trembling metal pipe   out into the
channels of the water meadow   forcing water into
roots   pasture to grow   keeping up the milk
yield   cash in the bank
sweet grass for the cows to wrap their rasping tongues
around   when moved into a fresh meadow they
rumble and dance   kick their legs in the air
udders flying like rubber gloves hanging on the washing
line in a sharp breeze   quick snatches of goodness
before standing under the willows ruminating   their
heads up   their eyes closed

I give the pump a proprietorial pat on its heaving sides
dip my fingers in the water   flick a blessing   walk
away whistling

54

steam rises off dung clogged lane   pushing behind
the murmuring herd on my quad bike in the mud
often as not with a child or two up beside me before
they're big enough for their own dirt bikes   as
contented as the cows waiting to be milked
I love my work   seventy-odd big-boned guernseys
placid as lake water   letting down their milk to the
tone of my voice   dairying is my life   all thought
of being a vet forgotten
deregulation the rough politics   prices uncertain
nearby factories build a reputation for good cheeses
I make sure my milk is what they want   a smooth-
running operation that makes money   keeps Mother
happy
and the cows   well the cows are like family to me

some farmwomen approach me to help set up a
dairywomen's association   an offshoot from the
Farmers' Federation   well me   imagine that!
so busy on the farm and with the kids and all   I
wouldn't have anything to say   but I join anyway
when it starts   don't get to meet many new people
interesting women too

55

when I first came to this farm   a green girl
I wouldn't say boo   not just because of my secret
because I knew by then that this was a silly reason to be
silent   I was quiet anyway and shy and uncertain and
pregnant   I was captivated   the land was lovely
in a perennially green valley   acres of pasture
and croplands and wooded hilltops   farm well-
established and big   no need to scrape and make do
I thought
the family well-established too   fourth generation
fifth with Dave and his brother Chris   I was
carrying the sixth generation   all that handing down
of knowledge would make a farm family wise and
generous   I thought

Dave's parents considered themselves above the migrant
families in the district   patronising hosts and
ungenerous   not popular   not particularly wise
either   as far as I could see   how come they had
such a nice son as Dave
I thought

56

other than the midwife and Meg and Rosy I found it hard to make friends   no home of my own to invite them to   conversations rushed at the school gate and tuckshop

it was refreshing to belong to an association of women with the same skills as me   I could feel my silence thawing

57

if I could speak out loud   speak my mind   if I
could just open my mouth and let words fall out
knowing that they would listen   if I could only say
what is on my mind but I can't
each has a voice which will be listened to but me
each can say their piece

58

Meg and Rosy know my secret   for years we have
met on a Friday morning at the Beechworth cafe
for years they have put up with my silences   for
years they have known I can talk but not the reason for
my silence   the telling is painful   they are angry
with John   but I have always been complicit   I
enjoyed it then   and have used the silence   and
continue to use it
Dave knows my secret   Meg and Rosy know my
secret   the family knows I can talk even if I
rarely do
how shall I break my silence with the world?

59

by the time the children are all at high school in
Tallangatta   Dave's losing his lovely red hair and
mine is needing some help   Dave's father gets more
tetchy by the day and Mother is doing some very
strange things   I wonder if dementia runs in the
family   goodness knows how we will manage if that
happens
with the kids filling their own days now I'm busier than
ever   and I get to thinking   as I'm asked to join
more farmwomen's organisations   I'm just as skilled
as anyone else on this farm   I love Dave dearly
but I'm as much a farmer as he is   I don't want to
push the point   he has such a tough time with his
dad   don't want to lower his self-confidence   he's
such a good solid farmer   careful with his decisions
and knowledgeable   I reckon I am too

IV

60

I am never bored   more things to do than waking hours   keep the Esse burning to feed nine people all day and again next morning   our clothes may not be new but they are always clean   no one going to school or college smelling of cow shit   I don't mind ironing   I enjoy cooking   I love my work in the dairy   I'm happy driving for spares and taxiing sons to footy   daughter to netball   growing vegies is not hard   I love to get my fingers in the dirt and see things grow

I move sprinklers all summer to keep things green

hard work never did anyone any harm   /*the Devil makes work for idle hands* my Gran used to say   but I'm just going to Gran I'd say   *the road to hell is paved with going to's*   she would retort   I think she taught me a good work habit   crabby old thing that she was/
I am intent on keeping the bookwork up-to-date and the mating charts and the mending and bottling and cutting everyone's hair while watching the ABC /we can't get those other stations in our valley/   and writing up the minutes of the farm meeting in which I have no voice   *but she can still write up the minutes can't she*
but Gran   *you* said actions speak louder than words

61

I drive the tractor whenever required   I don't get to
drive the header   that's men's business   I drive
the car a lot and the ute and the cattle truck and I drove
the grain truck one year when Dave had broken his
ankle and Chris had commandeered the header
air-conditioned and with CD stack   the grain
truck is not air-conditioned   is accessed through
the passenger door because the driver's door is so
battered by hitting the loading bay that it doesn't open
the grain truck holds twelve tonnes and really gets going
down to the silo   the truck has brakes that needed
replacing years ago but it doesn't get used much and
heck they'll last a bit longer   eh

the guys at the silo are not comfortable with women but
I don't talk to them so it doesn't matter that they don't
talk to me   it's like that at the stock and station
agents as well and the bank   and the field days
there are other farmwomen who fill in same as me

62

when the grain harvest is on   nasty things get said
and done in the blaze of anxiety   will we get it all in
before the break   will that cloud drop some rain
will the truck break down   will the header last
another season   will the price drop   /probably
it usually does/   a bumper crop and the market is
glutted   no rain for months and the stalks dwindle
and fry   a market in Russia opens up   trade talks
with the US shut it down   the tension building
and building and the heat oppressive
tempers boiling over little things   the brother-in-law
feels me up   the sister-in-law shouts at me and Sally
Dave almost cries when the truck blows a tyre on the
way to the silo
I don't feel like singing

63

he says it drives him mad   Dave's brother   my
brother-in-law   Chris says it drives him mad when I
don't answer him
when he gets hopping mad I have a little secret grin
he can't get at me in my silence   but I can get at him
but when he is cut away from under the rolled-over
grain truck   /it was just meanness   not getting
the brakes seen to/   when he is taken away I think it
is me that has made him mad   me that has caused
his frenzy   me that has caused his death   silence
is not golden

64

Dave is no longer the second son

65

sobering enough to lose a family member in such a shocking way   but when I see how they treat my sister-in-law   food for serious thought about my own position
my sister-in-law is told   not kindly   to find somewhere else to live
she discovers that there is no allowance made for her widowhood   that these two people whom I have to call Mother and Father are turning her out without a cent   Dave and I plead with them   even the children beg them to reconsider   the sister-in-law who I admire now more than at any time before   is too proud to grovel   takes them to court   the ensuing settlement is longwinded   grudging mean

66

Dave and I sit down one day with a community lawyer
in Wodonga   /not the family solicitor/   discuss
options to avoid this happening to us   unbiased
she advises us on succession planning   says such
matters are often neglected on family farms   not
really meanness she says   just anxiety about the
viability of the family farm   lots of tips and leaflets
and new ideas
getting through to the parents is not so simple   we'll
have to wait until they die

67

Mother has dementia   not just losing her glasses
losing her grip on reality   sad but funny almost
always so particular   now undone
don't know how much longer we can cope with her
certainly can't ask the sister-in-law to help
no aged-care facilities nearer than Tallangatta and they're
full to busting   country women in particular
strong and long-lived
Father   distressed   angry   unable to help her
he also frailer by the moment   often almost
catatonic with fury
Mother's on several waiting lists for nursing homes in

Wangaratta and Wodonga   waiting lists that often go
on until death   quite out of daily visiting range
she will lose herself as well as us
my own Dad growing old meekly under the thumb of
Aunt Ada   accepting rare visits of grandchildren with
apparent pleasure   gruff stories about the farm
never was one for talking

68

all of us getting older   Dave's curly red hair just a
wavy watermark on a shiny-brown skull   still a big
gentle bear of a man   still hardworking   making
his own decisions about a farm   which will one day
belong to him
Father keeps reminding him that it doesn't   yet

69

Robbie works in tandem with his dad   no shouting
between these two   it's good not to have to do so
many heavy things on the farm   time to dream up
alternative crops   persimmons maybe   chestnuts
even
Robbie's not quiet like his mum   not hot-headed
like his brother   not snobby like his grandparents
except for his red hair I'd say he's like my Dad   even
his hair is more sunset gold than carrot   and he's just
crazy about anything to do with farming and dirt bikes
and girls and footy   I think there's a bit of Irish in
him

70

Sam is off at uni in Brisbane learning to be what I
thought I wanted to be   a vet   /St Lucia the only
place he can study large animals/   inheriting his
dad's way with creatures but not his gentleness
flame tempered and temperamental   Sam doesn't
always come home for the holidays   he and his
Grandpa have always rubbed each other up the wrong
way   terrible sparring partners

71

my Sally growing more beautiful every day   Sally
loves high school   big boned   energetic   fiery
chestnut hair in curls that are usually scooped into a
ponytail   no ribbons or fuss for this one   a regular
tomboy   not silent like me   an outgoing child
and popular   with a total passion for agriculture
learning it like a trade
I'm not going to marry a farmer Mum
I'm going to be one!

72

Dad and Ada come out to visit from time to time
they never stopover   Mother and Father always go
out   they do it to be rude but we all enjoy
catching up with Dad while they're out   the children
are really fond of him   he and I are still awkward
and quiet with each other   I wonder if he is happy

73

when it rains in our valley   quite often   the grass greens and the cud sweetens   the milk flows and the grain inches up
I put on my black wellie boots and slick black oilies and my current beanie shining the maroon and gold colours of Robbie's footy team
I slip down the hillsides and slosh along the cow tracks singing into the mist
the milking takes longer in the rain   cows reluctant to leave sweet pasture   dung and mud clinging to their tails   flanks   hooves   their udders plastered   the dairy and yard filthy   the run-off water a rich sludgy brown

I take the user-friendly quad bike up into the forest
I feel safer on the four dumpy wheels of the quad than
on a dirt bike   leave those for the young   great
views where the forestry workers have clear-felled
out to the Riverina between the rain squalls   chink
and clank of bellbirds where the native regrowth has
been left   water dripping from long eucalypt leaves
down the neck of my Drizabone
it keeps me out of the house   dark on rainy days and
overfull   all of them eating nonstop to fill the dreary
can't work hours

much better to sing in the rain

74

when I'm up there   feels like on top of the world
I look out over the land which I love   I think about
the Aborigines who once lived here   did they too sit
on these hilltops and survey their land with pride
did we steal it from them?   I'd like to ask them but
there are no Aboriginal women in our farmwomen
groups   they've been invited but don't come
maybe they never thought of themselves as farmers
maybe they don't feel welcome
I've never met an Aborigine face to face   got to be
careful what I say at home   *we paid for this land*
we've worked for what we've got
not racist exactly

75

this family belongs to the land which has been farmed
by them for five generations   they belong to the
local church and hold positions in it   think of
themselves as good Christians
across the generations men have been councillors
one a mayor even
women have taken prizes at the local Agricultural Show
for their alarmingly tall sponge cakes and their
decorative bottled vegetables and their cross-stitch and
their dairy cows
dead they are buried in the local cemetery
even in death they belong here
I live on this farm but I do not belong   other
women have lived on this farm who were not born here
did they belong?
maybe I have to speak up   to belong

76

where do I belong?
the children   /hardly children any more/
belong to the farm family and this community   they
were born here
the cows belong to the herd   they have a leader and
hangers on   they each know their place and stick to
it   I don't know my place and if I do   I don't
want to stick to it   I don't want out   I want to be
more in the family   more in the farm   more in
the world   if I talked about Uncle John   I'm
afraid of being laughed at   they'd be so taken aback
at me talking let alone talking about that
my voice belongs to Uncle John   and I want it back

77

how did she know?   she's never heard me sing
you old witch Rosy   catching me off guard like that
I thought singing was my own secret   the way it
makes my heart zing and blat and dance a jig   the
way the cows let down their milk when I sing to them
softly they murmur to me like they do to their newborn
calves   mother-love songs of welcome and recognition
they murmur and let down their milk   it's supposed
to be a secret Rosy

will I join her choir?   I'll have to ask Dave   but
he doesn't do anything on a Wednesday night   likes
to watch TV   I don't know
she says there's no audition   all women singing
without accompaniment she says   *a capella* she calls it
how did she know?
that Rosy!

78

can't think why I've been silent for so long   I
love singing in the choir   women's songs and songs
about peace not war and about Mandela and Chile and
love and songs for sons and daughters and songs about
the goddess even whoever she may be   I don't always
understand but that doesn't matter   it makes me
happy   I don't think I knew I wasn't happy but now
I think perhaps I wasn't   quite

not unhappy with Dave or farming or anything   but
now I have a voice   maybe I can speak up at family
farm meetings

79

it's just for me   wonderful Wednesday nights just for me   no family here   no one who knows me except Rosy   and I can sing out loud   I can sing

80

so wonderful to have a voice   and not just at singing
at dairywomen's meetings too and at Women in
Agriculture
I find I'm an outgoing person just like Sally
time to learn new skills at TAFE with other farmwomen
learning to call ourselves farmers   not just farmers'
wives   farm bookkeeping   computer skills
networking   I'm no feminist but I can see that us
women need to have more input into government
not politics as such   but policy making   policies
made by people who know what's needed out here on
farms   like safe child care   aged-care facilities
I think I want to do a company director's course
Dave is excited about my getting so involved   really
supportive   mind you   I haven't opened up yet at
the farm meetings   they'll get a shock when I do

81

in summer   the wind blowing sour from the
desolate north   smelling of offal and blowflies and
the bitter muskiness of long-dead dried-out cattle
carcasses and roadkill   the sun searing the sweat
off my skin   eating its way into my soul   burning
my mousy hair bright white   my plump pink arms
brown as the Italian women cutting apricots on the
fruit blocks in the Riverina   in summer the
milking takes less time   the cows drowsy in the sun
the tanker through with his round in half the time
in summer I can work on my own crops   no one
else to make decisions for me   picking the tiny
gherkins daily   /wading through the prickly
green watery leaves   stooping again and again
riffling my fingers through dark secrets
always finding my booty   day after day after
sunny day/   the pleasure of the trip into the

factory   the cash into my own purse and into the Commonwealth savings account that no one but me has access to   I don't know what I'm saving for

no matter how hot   in summer I pick gherkins and strawberries and potatoes and beans   carrots parsnips   onions   zucchinis   parsley and basil and oregano and thyme   apricots nectarines peaches plums and olives   asparagus   artichokes rhubarb   when I'm through picking I put the sprinklers back on the vegie patch and listen to it all growing again

82

in summer I bottle and make jam   I pickle freeze and cook   apricot crumble and zucchini cakes and pickled onions and glazed baby carrots and basil pesto and lemon and thyme stuffing for home-killed meat chook and quince jelly to drown in the hollows of Yorkshire pudding and rich tomato sauce brightening our own beef mince   and with the wood stove still blasting heat the family sits around the kitchen table and scoffs the lot   but I have the pleasure in the making

83

it was a terrible misunderstanding   I should have said something but it was left to simmer and now my poor boy
at one of the family farm meetings   my Sam said he didn't want to come to the meetings anymore   he'd been offered a place as a junior partner in a veterinary practice in Myrtleford specialising in large animals /what he had trained for/   he was so proud

you would have thought the end of the world had come Dave's dad   /Father we all still call him/   sprang to his feet red in the face and bulging eyes and shouted hoarsely   *never!   never in a thousand years!   the eldest son always works the farm   have I done all this*

work and my father and his before him to see you throw it away?   never!
he didn't swear   he never did   he didn't have to
what he said   went
no more was said

84

so the young hot-head took his Grandpa's gun   no
way anyone could pretend it was an accident   into
the hayloft above the dairy   and he propped the gun
on a hay bale and cocked it with twine   it had a hair
trigger he knew   he had shot rabbits with it any
number of times   he was twenty-two and knew what
he was doing   he sat on another hay bale in the line
of fire   and he pulled
we heard the explosion from the kitchen   who was
out shooting tonight?
when I found him in the hay I screamed   oh no my
boy Sam no   I got blood all over me   his blood
as I kissed him

but most of the wet was tears   *I wanted to end it all*
Mum he wailed in my arms   thank the Lord the hay
bale shifted as he pulled   he missed   the blood
was a graze along his cheekbone
this close to permanent silence

85

having recently questioned my own happiness   I
never thought to question my children's   I have
always found family meetings irksome   with no
voice   they must have tortured Sam   maybe Chris
even
living with Father so many years   I know his tyranny
as one-eyed concern for the family farm
my Sam's misery is hard for me to bear   the farm
splits my loyalty
Sam has made his escape   not the way he planned
months of difficult psychotherapy   his lovely red hair
gone snow white with the shock   gone to start afresh
in Queensland

86

how I need my friends   Meg stayed lanky and now greying and tall she looks quietly elegant   she has taught all of my kids chemistry yet through all the difficult years she remains calm and efficient   and such a dear friend
Rosy has had her wild moments   has done things neither Meg nor I would dare   travelled through India on her own   gone ballooning in Arizona with a handsome but morally-questionable man from an enormous ranch in Texas   married and divorced three husbands   picked up and adopted a gorgeous girl child in Burma another in Bali and twin boys in Samoa   all four of them now swelling the ranks of our threatened two-teacher primary school as they live in happy chaos in a run-down vacant farm house down the road
Rosy sweeps everybody off their feet
I wish I was more like Rosy

87

promised time and time again I'll dig out those water
colours   gift from Aunt Ada   must be fifteen years
ago   she's dead now   Dad alone again   as I
stand outside the dairy   waiting for Robbie on his
mud-slathered dirt bike bringing in the cows   I
promise myself I'll paint the way the rays of the sun
angle up over the hillside behind the homestead
magic and unreal like some health advert in a woman's
magazine   then spread sparkling fanwise until the
sun's up and I can't look any more   even squinting
and the cows are here anyway but my heart feels like
busting
the pleasure of it
above me two wedge-tailed eagles float circling

circling on the thermals   couldn't I just get that lazy
flight above the clear-felled hills   the dark forest
up   up   the tops of the trees flame orange in the
break of day sunlight
the light   movement   the colour   paint to
brush   brush to paper   if I had the time

88

it was tiny   just the size of a split pea   Dave found
it   I never would have   too busy dealing with
cows tits to think of my own   but as soon as Dave
found it I felt invaded   I was frightened   so was
Dave
embarrassed when I had to lower my bra for the local
GP to feel it   he said have your breasts always been
lopsided?   *ask Dave* I should have said but of course I
didn't   that was the first embarrassment of many
after surgery   /with one breast smaller and lighter
than the other if not lopsided/   I am calmed by
nurses who seem to know more than doctors

89

no local hospital   we did have one before the
'eighties   only used for emergencies now
broken wrists   bee stings   things that the sister
can deal with
for anything serious it's the base hospital one hundred
kilometres away and think yourself lucky not to have to
go to Melbourne
when I've had the operation   lying stiff and sore on
my rubber-sheeted bed   wide awake with the
constant noise
before I see the doctor I wonder if this is it   my
allotted time   how will they manage without me?
I worry and retch and retch and worry until I'm sedated
afterwards when he says *we got it all* I recognise my
arrogance but it took a while

Rosy visits me each day   a quick hug and sparkling
conversation   Rosy knowing my silence   Rosy
always sparkles   Rosy is such a good friend   I love
them all but am tired   so tired
this is my first holiday since our honeymoon
strange to be sleeping alone   strange to have nothing
to do
that bloody hayloft is always in my mind   always in
my mind
I should have broken my silence at that meeting and said
something to support Sam

90

Meg has me to stay for a couple of days   *too lively at Rosy's*   she murmurs   *and they'll have you working if you go home*
I wander round Meg's tidy house   one person with a house all to oneself   how would it be   playing the piano   reading novels   having friends to dinner   hard to imagine   I've never done these things
do I miss them?   I haven't   until now

Saturday afternoon Meg gets on her gardening gear and reaches for an old cotton hat   says *I'm off to a Landcare meeting   d'you feel up to coming?*

I've known Meg nearly all my life and hers
how come I hardly know her?

I would have asked you to join   says Meg quietly as we
drive home   *but I knew you would say you had no time
to spare*

91

Meg told me the talk was of nothing but sludge pumps
the first year she went to Landcare   all men of course
when local farmwomen started taking an interest they
rolled up their sleeves for some serious
environmentalism   involving the whole school
community   using school gardening and computer
facilities   getting good speakers to explain ridge
ploughing for waterless planting of native species
keyline irrigation   fauna conservation
the men still go to the front bar to talk about sludge
pumps

92

when I came home   good thing I didn't expect them
to make allowances and the milk yield had sunk into the
subsoil
scared me though   and I thought it was only stressed
people who got cancer

93

cancer helped me see the world differently   at the
time I was just fighting to survive   to stay in a world
I was not ready to leave
but now   I see that I work hard to be a good
dairywoman but the farming world sees only dairymen
I see there's more to a feminist stance than meets the eye
and I don't need to be afraid of it
I see my children and their mates not convinced by
outdated assumptions
farmers make many mistakes   politicians make many
mistakes on our behalf   I have made many mistakes
I see John was mistaken
I do not need to keep his secret any more

94

when my Dad died   not that long ago   bent with
hard work and puzzled by a world he had not expected
to know   when Dad died he had outlasted both his
wives so he left his estate to me   but his estate was
not our farm   that was long ago sold because there
was no son to inherit
when Dad died he was so old there wasn't much estate
left   he'd lived it   what was left was poured
straightaway into the bottomless hole that is the family
farm   *what's yours is his*   /and what's his is his
too by their standards/
I did get Dad's treasured fountain pen engraved
with his own name the same as his father's and his old
farm ledgers which are comfortingly terse

cleared new paddock
crop down must have been that late hard frost
mechanic repaired thresher it went again first time round the paddock
rain'd better stop   creek overflowing   sheep drowning
girl child   hard calving   won't be any more doctor says
paddock full of parrots eating seed
bumper crop —   cleared mortgage
why has the child stopped talking?
I loved her chatter   was it John?

I never knew it bothered him

95

I was uncertain about Landcare   *greenie* in our valley
far ruder than dumbo   even farmers growing
plantation blue gum careful to avoid confrontation
there's a huge pride that bolsters the agriculture of this
country   a willful pride that says this is the way it's
been done for generations   if it was good enough
then
all the same   there's head scratching at lowering
yields and weed infestations and foxes and spray
resistance and phytopthera and trade barriers and
removal of tariffs and ticks and heartworm and BSE
and CJD and foot and mouth   lots of head
scratching and opportunities for government
inspectors and young men straight out of college
calling themselves agricultural experts and even

the stock and station agents now   always a farmer's
best friend   even them   talking about leaving old-
growth forest   natural ecosystems   genetic
modification   alternative crops and
going to Landcare would set me against the family

96

you stupid dumb woman you'll bring fire down the valley
vermin   parrots will eat all our crops
but the fire has gone out of him   out like the fire in
the eyes of his spiteful wife   dead these two blissful
years   Robbie and his dad are making decisions now
and he can only watch and rant   apoplexy closing in
I go up into the forest to collect seeds of the mountain
pepper   river peppermint   messmate and red box
yellow gum   silver wattle and eastern leatherwood
lay out the trays   water carefully   prick out the
sharp-odoured seedlings into used pots

Robbie and a fencing contractor put in new fence lines
new gates   deep rip ready for dry planting   I'll be
a grandmother before it's finished   it'll change the
face of this farm

97

she'll only marry a farmer   why send her to agricultural college?   in my day they wouldn't let females do such things and quite right too
my Sally   big-boned and tanned   her curly red hair in a pony tail bounces as she strides around the farm   she always strides   she always wears jeans
blooming with health and vitality   she makes me feel old and tired but she's lovely   Father expects her to settle down and breed
Sally has other ideas but he won't take any notice   he took no notice of what Sam wanted   my Sam   so far away

Sam's not spoken of now at farm meetings and Father's
will says that Robbie will inherit in line from his father
nothing for Sal though   she's a girl
at least we can change all that in our own wills   but
not until the old man dies   I don't see why being a
girl means you can't inherit   neither do her brothers
she so much wants to farm   she'll do well at Dookie
Ag College

98

I know that Sally and her girlfriend Steff are saving like
crazy   both of them working all hours of the day and
night   they've got their eye on a little farm over the
mountain   good water   good pasture   belongs
to an old bachelor in his nineties   they want to run
bobby calves and grow persimmons   good luck to
them I say   I loved growing up in the hill country
I think they'll have a hard time   not a tolerant district

my children have given me such pleasure
          when I first realised   that Sal might
not have children it made me sad   but all Dave and I
want is her happiness   she sees no need to be
silent
not about loving women   not about farming   not
about succession   not about anything really
but there's no way she will come out to her grandfather

99

the way he says that about Sal   makes me see red
not like me   not usually a hot-head
I've always avoided conflict and communed with my
cows   got enough red-headed hot-heads in this
family without me   but I see
red   in front of the whole family
/*got out the wrong side of bed she did*   my Gran would
have said/

I yell at him   him and his family farm and his
precious inheritance   him and his firstborn
son and firstborn grandson   his firstborn son
is dead I say and my husband has always done
all the work round here   he has driven Sam away

so far away   yet Robbie and Sally want only to farm
can't you see what you have done to this family
shrieking now   *you wicked old man*
my hand to my mouth
I sit down suddenly
the silence in the farm kitchen is complete

100

silent tears stain his weathered face   *the farm*   he stutters   *the farm*
I go and stand behind him   my arms round his hunched shoulders   I lay my grey head against his white mop   run my wet nose through his hair weep silently with him   croon at an old man I have humbled

I make us all a cup of tea   Dave comes up behind me at the woodstove   his arms right round me cupping my breasts   in front of everyone   whispers *I'm so proud of you*
I turn into his arms

101

the farm family has been so trapped in our own little world   so caught up in the business of farming everything we do revolves around us and our farm   our land   our inheritance   and passing it on in the right way to the right son and doing everything the way it has always been done

heading for a quiet revolution   maybe

V

102

I put down my name to represent farmwomen on
boards   any boards but mainly agricultural   I'm
asked to be community rep on the syllabus board for
the ag science department at the Wodonga campus of
the university
they meet in the Senate Room round a table bigger
than our milk vat   with arm chairs   water jugs
gold-framed dignitaries staring down at us   all men
of course
Dr This and Professor That don't ask who I am
they don't even look at me while quoting figures
bottom lines   and quality assurance

I'm just a dairy farmer   I am overawed by my first
board meeting   by the Senate Room   by the men
in suits   until they rise to leave when I break my
silence
in a small woman's voice that carries across the paddock
to call in the cows I say *what is the agricultural content of
your course?*
in the icy silence they sit back down   they look at
me   I hold their gaze and ask again *what are you
teaching our sons and daughters?*
but they don't know and I come away knowing us
farmwomen must sit on more boards

103

they can't stop me talking   about dairying and
forestry
agripolitics and content of agricultural courses   about
fishing rights and value-adding   farmstay and tourism
about Women in Agriculture and women at farm
gatherings   conferences about the future of rural
women   workshops on succession planning
lobbying in Canberra   last year I was named Rural
Woman of the Year for the state   nominated by the
dairywomen's group for my new methods of rearing
bobby calves   what a way to start the new
millennium   this year I got a Dairyfarmers'
scholarship to go to a worldwide conference of
farmwomen in Spain   Dave came too and Robbie

had all responsibility for the farm   first time either
of us had been overseas   there were fifteen hundred
farmwomen at the Spanish conference
so many new experiences   farming gets more and
more exciting as I get older   and since I have broken
my silence I talk   talk with   talk to anybody
who'll stand still for long enough   one of these days
someone is going to tell me to shut up

104

Dave and Robbie and I don't need to add more land to the farm   got more than enough already   our contribution to this family farm   /now we can speak for ourselves/   is to carry through on new ideas for the land we have   high fat content for cheese   strong breeding stock   careful water management   safe ponies for children   fine Merino wool   grain that crops well whatever the weather   we're good farmers and we love our land

105

when I was a little girl I was violated by Uncle John but didn't recognise it as such   I was not his victim but my voice was

a young girl   I was wronged by my father when he sold the farm but didn't recognise it as such   my Sally is finding her own way around the dilemma of primogeniture

as a pregnant wife I was not welcomed into the family but have served them well

my children have broken the family mold but still have a way forward in the world   two farmers' children Dave and me   have produced two more good farmers and a vet   with a deep respect for the land

I have found my voice

106

when I get a good price at auction for a hand-raised
weaner   I think *yes*   and when I plant out a
windbreak of indigenous trees along the curve of the
paddock   I think *yes*   and when I make a batch
of strawberry jam that sets without pectin and when my
latest sketch gets hung in an exhibition
when my daughter buys her own farm and when I pass
a TAFE course with Distinction at forty-nine   when
my own specialty chooks take champion at the local
show and my persimmons that everyone laughed at
fetch top price at the Melbourne wholesale market
I think *yes* for farmwomen
and for me too   *yes*   I have a voice   now I
do belong

I am a farmer

107

I can speak out loud   speak my mind